THE MERCER CURSE

The Mercer Curse

*Prequel to
The Jewelry Box Series*

by

New York Times Bestseller
Pepper Winters

The Mercer Curse
Copyright © 2024 Pepper Winters
Published by Pepper Winters

All rights reserved. No part of this book may be reproduced or transmitted in any form, including electronic or mechanical, without written permission from the publisher, except in the case of brief quotations embodied in critical articles or reviews.

This is a work of fiction. Names, characters, businesses, places, events, and incidents are either the products of the author's imagination or used in a fictitious manner. Any resemblance to actual persons, living or dead, or actual events is purely coincidental.

This book is licensed for your personal enjoyment only. This book may not be re-sold or given away to other people. If you would like to share this book with another person, please purchase an additional copy for each person you share it with. If you are reading this book and did not purchase it, or it was not purchased for your use only, then you should return it to the seller and purchase your own copy. Libraries are exempt and permitted to share their in-house copies with their members and have full thanks for stocking this book. Thank you for respecting the author's work.

Published: Pepper Winters 2023: pepperwinters@gmail.com
Cover Design: Pepper Winters
Proofread by: Christina Routhier
French Translation: Aurelie Gordio
Audio Narration: Luke William Bromley and Lucy Jessica
Ebook Cover: Cleo Designs
Paperback Cover: Cleo Designs
Hardback Image: Julia Cherrett Valareign (etsy)
Internal pages images: Julia Cherrett Valareign (etsy)

OTHER WORK BY PEPPER WINTERS

Pepper currently has close to forty books released in nine languages. She's hit best-seller lists (USA Today, New York Times, and Wall Street Journal) almost forty times. She dabbles in multiple genres, ranging from Dark Romance, Coming of Age, Fantasy, and Romantic Suspense.

For books, FAQs, and buylinks please visit:

https://pepperwinters.com

Subscribe to New Release Newsletter by following QR code

EROTIC 'SPECTACLE OF SECRETS' STANDALONES

One Dirty Night
(Ella and Nicholas)
One Arranged Night
(Vivian and Alasdair - 2024)
One Broken Night
(To be advised)
One Complicated Night
(To be advised)

FORBIDDEN ROMANCE

The Luna Duet
Lunamare (Book One of The Luna Duet)
Cor Amare (Book Two of The Luna Duet)

DARK ROMANCE

Goddess Isles Series
Once a Myth
Twice a Wish
Third a Kiss
Fourth a Lie
Fifth a Fury

Monsters in the Dark Trilogy
Tears of Tess
Quintessentially Q
Twisted Together
Je Suis a Toi

Indebted Series
Debt Inheritance
First Debt
Second Debt
Third Debt
Fourth Debt
Final Debt
Indebted Epilogue

Dollar Series
Pennies
Dollars
Hundreds
Thousands
Millions

Fable of Happiness Trilogy
Book One
Book Two
Book Three

SEXY ROMANCE

The Master of Trickery Duet
The Body Painter
The Living Canvas

Truth & Lies Duet

Crown of Lies
Throne of Truth

COMING OF AGE LOVE STORY

The Ribbon Duet
The Boy & His Ribbon
The Girl & Her Ren

Standalone Spinoff
The Son & His Hope

STANDALONES

Destroyed – Grey Romance
Unseen Messages – Survival Romance
One Dirty Night – Erotic Romance
Can't Touch This – Romantic Comedy

MOTORCYCLE CLUB ROMANCE

Pure Corruption Duet
Ruin & Rule
Sin & Suffer

ROMANTIC COMEDY written as TESS HUNTER

Can't Touch This

CHILDREN'S / INSPIRATIONAL BOOK

Pippin and Mo

FANTASY ROMANCE

Destini Chronicles
When a Moth Loved a Bee (Book One)
And a Bee Dared to Die (Book Two)
Book Two is currently on hold but will be advised at a later date.

UPCOMING RELEASES

For 2024/2025 titles please visit www.pepperwinters.com

RELEASE DAY ALERTS, SNEAK PEEKS, & NEWSLETTER
To be the first to know about upcoming releases, please join Pepper's Newsletter (she promises never to spam or annoy you.)

Pepper's Newsletter

SOCIAL MEDIA & WEBSITE
Facebook: Peppers Books
Instagram: @pepperwinters
Facebook Group: Peppers Playgound
Website: www.pepperwinters.com
Tiktok: @pepperwintersbooks

DEDICATION

To those who love a little pain with their pleasure…

CHAPTER ONE

"*MAÎTRE?*"

I groaned and squeezed the back of my neck.

Whenever she called me that, bad things happened.

Hot, dark, deliciously bad things.

"*Esclave*...I told you. Give me thirty minutes and then I'll fuck you within an inch of your life. *Distrais-moi et tu saigneras pour cette erreur.*" (Distract me and you'll be bleeding for the mistake.)

The soft whispers of her bare feet on carpet sounded behind me. "I haven't come for you to pleasure or punish me, Master."

"Oh?" I ran my fingers over the figures of the latest building development in Amsterdam. "Why are you here then? Corrupting me like you always do..."

She didn't reply, creeping up behind me like a girl who wanted to provoke every despicable monster that lived within me.

I shuddered.

I felt the darkness unfurl and get ready to play.

The short leash I kept myself on had ensured I'd lived a lonely, miserable existence before Tess tripped over my doorstep, spat with such intoxicating fury, and ensured I tumbled right into the darkness with her.

She was the only slave I'd ever touched.

The only woman I'd ever loved.

The only mate I wanted, now and forever.

Doing my best to ignore her games, I kept my gaze on the spreadsheet. I'd been offered the deal by a middle-ranking Dutch Mafia member—a bastard who thought he could go behind his bosses and make some coin on the side by enticing me and my overly inflated bank account.

Pity for him, I knew exactly what he was and cast out my line, fishing with bait I knew he wouldn't be able to refuse.

I'd said I needed a special sort of incentive to work with him.

He'd laughed and told me to meet him in the red-light district.

I'd gone, purely because I'd heard rumours. And rumours always started in truth. He dabbled in slavery. Sold living, breathing girls and boys as if they were coins to buy him power.

It was up to me to see if that was true.

And do something about it if it was.

Despite my wife's fury, I'd flown to Amsterdam three days ago. I'd allowed the bastard to seduce and flatter me, but the moment he'd closed the hotel suite's door and paraded a whimpering sixteen-year-old girl shot to hell with heroin toward me, he'd signed his death warrant.

The girl was a gift.

For me.

Like always.

My reputation preceded me in almost every country on this godforsaken planet.

Police knew who I was.

Criminals knew who I was.

Both of them had a different story, truth mixed with lies, and neither of them were the wiser.

I'd swallowed down my rage as the broken, skinny girl stumbled toward me. I'd allowed her to crumple at my feet and pretended to listen to the bastard's demands.

I would've killed him right there but…he wasn't the only one trying to forge this alliance. Instead of giving into my bloodlust, I kept my smile in place, accepted the girl, and flew her back to my estate in France on my private plane.

His death would come…once I knew how many other girls he had and where I could find them.

Tess hadn't blinked an eye as I carried yet another slave into our marital home. She merely summoned Suzette, told Mrs Sucre to get cooking, and Franco pushed open a door to one of the fifty guest rooms for this purpose as I strode through opulence and tucked the drugged-up girl into safety.

The doctor had come.

Two days into the girl's detox and she'd finally stopped screaming. She'd now turned catatonic instead.

"You haven't touched me since you returned from Amsterdam," Tess murmured as she pushed me back in my chair and deliberately sat her pretty ass on my desk, squashing my paperwork. "You went without my permission. You put yourself in danger. You made me mad, Q Mercer, and you know what happens when you do that."

I smirked and reclined. "Remind me, wife…what happens when I make you mad?"

"I make you lose your mind."

My blood heated. "And what is your plan tonight, *esclave*? How are you planning on making me come undone?" My hand dropped between my legs, fisting the hard-on she caused every time I caught her scent. "Because I will be coming…whether you will too is a matter of discussion."

"Oh, you'll make me come, husband. You won't have a

choice."

I chuckled and stroked myself. "Bold, Tess. Very bold."

"You left me." Her hands went to the belt holding her satiny, sexy dressing gown closed. The faint lilac gown had looked stunning on its hanger in the lingerie shop in Amsterdam, but on her?

She made it fucking sinful.

"You brought home another woman." She unthreaded the bow, letting the material slip like water from her delectable skin. Skin I'd marked, bit, branded, and whipped. Skin that bloomed a perfect shade of red. Skin that always healed so I could do it all over again.

A tremor ran through me as my cock hit full mast, growing painful in my slacks. With steady hands, I reached for my belt.

Her eyes shot to where I unhooked the leather, no doubt remembering the many times I'd had her spread over my desk, her hips in the air, and the crack of my belt landing against her ass.

"Go on…" I whispered, my French accent thickening like it always did when she tempted me. "Tell me why I should tolerate you being mad at me for saving yet another slave and doing what I must to repent for what I am."

"What you are?" With a shudder, she spread her legs, planting her heels on my rock-hard thighs. "What you are is *mine*. My monster. And I want to get mauled." The gown fell away, leaving swathes of skin from collarbone to pussy. The swell of her breasts teased me, the Q branded over her heart enraged me, the inked sparrows flying over her shoulder undid me, and the wetness glimmering between her thighs fucking broke me.

I groaned. "*Je vais me régaler de toi, ma femme.*" (I'm going to feast on you, wife).

"Promise?" Her hand trailed down her belly, heading south.

Unzipping my slacks, I pulled my cock out, digging my thumb painfully into the tip. I couldn't look away as she swirled her clit. Her long, wavy blonde hair cascaded over her shoulders, the soft light from my desk lamp caping her in shadows and secrets.

Tess had always been beautiful. Even when she'd broken my black fucking heart, she'd been the most stunning creature I'd ever seen.

But now that she was my wife?

Now that she was mine in every way—blooded, bonded, and betrothed…I couldn't look at another woman without comparing them. Comparing their strength to hers. Their light to hers. Her ability to make me feel when everyone else in the world made me shut down.

"Don't you want a taste, *maître*?"

"*Merde*." My heart pounded. My ears rushed with white noise. I wanted her moaning in pleasure and screaming in pain. I wanted to hug her and hurt her at the same time. I wanted her blood on my tongue and her cum on my fingers. I both loved and hated her. Her power. Her fight. Her undeniable claim over me.

The one girl who'd come to me unbroken.

The one girl to break me in return.

She moaned as her finger dipped inside. The nightgown darkened beneath her ass with her need.

Swallowing hard, I growled, "If you get that paperwork wet, you're in trouble."

Moaning, she tipped her head back. "You know what your threats do to me."

"Fuck yes, I do." I shot up from my chair, fisting my cock with one hand and snatching her hip with the other. Yanking her to the edge of the desk, paper fluttered to the floor, but I didn't give a fuck.

Tess deserved to pay for making me this senseless. She needed another endless night in chains while I did whatever I damn well wanted to her.

I wanted to taste.

But not the part of her she was expecting.

Grabbing the sharp letter opener glinting by my lamp, I dropped my head between her thighs. The scent of her arousal made a ripple of need work up my cock. She always did this to me. Made me too eager. Too willing to blur the lines between husband and beast.

Her breath turned thin and quick as I blew a stream of air on her clit.

"Q. Yes. God, please..."

Keeping my eyes locked on the most vulnerable part of her—the part no one else would ever see or touch unless they wanted to have their heart ripped out by my bare hands—I dragged the letter opener along the inside of her trembling thigh.

She stiffened at the sharpness.

She stopped breathing as I dug the point into the crease where her pussy met her leg. Such a delicate place. Paper thin skin, easily damaged, and beautifully bruised with spiderwebs of arteries and veins.

"You couldn't give me an hour to finish, *esclave*? You had to come and interrupt me."

"I missed you."

"I wouldn't admit that if I were you." I dipped my head and ran my tongue from her wet entrance to her tight little clit. "I'll get a god complex."

"Don't care." She shuddered as I nipped her, dragging my tongue back to her entrance, my hand tightening around the letter opener as a flush of her desire coated my lips.

"You don't care that I hold your life in my hands?" I bit her again, making her cry out. "You don't care that I get off knowing I could so easily hurt you?"

She squirmed on my desk, locking onto the two words that'd become an awful aphrodisiac between us. Between a sadist and his masochist. Between two monsters who'd found each other in the dark.

"Hurt me," she breathed.

"I thought you'd never ask." I fell on her pussy, lapping up every drop of need, biting, laving, driving my tongue as deep as it would go. Her moans came quick with intoxicating gasps.

I let her think I would take her to the edge. That I would let her come on my tongue. Her legs clenched, her toes dug into my thighs where she still had her feet planted. Her moans turned to whimpers. The first squeeze of her pussy around my tongue—

Ripping my face from her, I soared upright and pressed the letter opener right over her jugular.

My cock speared up, sticking out from my suit. I was fully dressed, and my Tess was naked on an altar to be eaten. So pretty. So pure. So perfect.

My teeth ached to bite. My tongue burned to taste.

Her eyes met mine with a flash of condemning black fire that also burned inside me. Fire that only grew hotter the longer we played.

Ever so slowly, she turned her head, surrendering her throat to me, giving me every shred of trust and submission. "Do it."

My lips pulled back as I traced her vein with the small stationery dagger.

My black heart pounded. My lips, still coated in her desire, stung for a different sort of flavour. One far more intimate than sexual pleasure. One of sickness and depravity. One that I needed to sate because her blood was my temporary cure. A shot of medicine to restrain myself for another day.

I didn't look away from her as I pressed the dagger just a little harder.

She flinched and moaned.

Everything inside me froze into predatory stillness as the first bead of ruby welled on her throat. The colour. The glisten. Her lifeforce and very essence.

Fuck.

Crushing her into my desk, I rocked my cock through her drenched folds as my mouth latched onto the droplet.

The moment her sweet, metallic, hot, hot blood soaked onto my tongue, I snapped.

She wanted to be fucked?

She just got her wish.

"Spread," I snarled, pushing her knees as wide as they'd go.

Lying back on my desk, her hair strewn over my laptop and other junk, she presented herself to me.

Tossing the letter opener away, my eyes locked on another droplet of crimson as it welled down her skin, down and down, coming to a stop in the hollow of her collarbone.

Fuck.

Me.

Dragging her hips the final inch off the desk, I sucked in a haggard breath. "Who are you, *esclave*?"

Her stunning smile glinted with sharp canines. "*La vôtre. Je suis à toi.*" (Yours. I'm yours).

My vision shot black.

I notched inside her.

I thrust.

The sensation of her body closing hot and wet around mine made all the blackness, all the wickedness, all the perversion inside me snarl.

I wanted to break her apart as I withdrew and plunged back in.

I wanted her screaming my name in both pleasure and pain.

My mouth locked over that little droplet of blood. Cooler, less viscous, already beginning to congeal.

I lost myself to her.

Fucking her against my desk, I snatched her jaw and planted my lips over hers.

I groaned as her tongue instantly stroked mine. Fierce

and snake-fast, she met me with war and violence.

The desk creaked as I turned manic.

The sounds of our flesh slapping together was a perfect melody.

Something crashed to the floor; I didn't care.

Tess's moans turned to animalistic grunts; I rejoiced.

My own roar built louder and louder in my belly the longer I drove myself deeper and deeper into my wife, punishing her, remembering her, eradicating any distance of the past few days.

Her breakable hands landed on my cheeks as I fucked her like I despised her. Her nails dug into my five o'clock shadow, threatening to draw my blood just like I'd drawn hers.

We were sick.

We were contagious.

We were free in this cage of our own making.

"Fuck, Tess. I can't—"

"Come. Come, *maître*."

It was her job to obey me. Her purpose to submit. But in that moment, she was my master and I let go.

The sharp, shooting waves of a release jettisoned out of me and into her. Splashing deep, wake after wake, full of bone-snapping pleasure.

Her hand shot between her legs, rubbing herself as I watched my cock spear in and out of her.

With a scream, she shattered, milking me in thick, erotic pulses, dragging out my own release until we both collapsed onto the desk.

Her bare chest panted beneath my suit-covered one. I pressed a worshipping kiss to the small wound I'd caused. "*Je t'aime*, Tess. With all my heart."

She stretched beneath me, making my cock hit different parts of her. "I love you too. With every part of me."

I kissed her sweetly, reverently.

What did I do to deserve this minx?

How had I been lucky enough to marry this wonderful woman?

Whatever it was, I was grateful. So fucking grateful she was mine.

My evening of work faded beneath images of taking her to our bedroom and pulling out the toy chest. I'd cuff her to the foot of the bed and—

"Eh, *maître?*"

Ah, fucking hell.

Having Tess call me her master made me ready to rut like a beast. Having my staff call me their master sent cold water of reality dousing over me.

I glowered over my shoulder.

Suzette stood with her back to the open door, her maid uniform pressed and neat like always. Clearly, she'd seen Tess spread half-naked with my cock impaled inside her, but I didn't try to cover up or explain.

She'd seen far worse.

All of our staff had.

Because...our household was unique.

Tess and I's relationship wasn't explainable to outsiders yet those who lived with us accepted us. They were trustworthy. They were our friends...family.

No one blinked an eye if Tess appeared at breakfast with teeth marks on her throat or crawled beneath the table at the snap of my fingers for her to suck me.

It'd taken a while to accept that they wouldn't judge who I was. And even longer to indulge in my deviant appetites.

But now, nothing could stop me because...I was happy.

I was fucking *happy* even with scum running around in the world. Buying and trading, kidnapping and trafficking. Scum that would one day die by my hand or someone else's. Scum that I used to believe lived inside me until Tess showed me I only wanted to kill her because she was my mirroring piece. My reflection of depravity. My monster just like I was hers.

"Not now, Suzette," Tess moaned and flopped her wrist over her forehead like some frustrated damsel. "Can't you see we're a little busy?"

Suzette's soft laughter came from the hallway. "I did see and I can't unsee, *mon ami*. But…Q is needed downstairs. There's someone here to see him."

"What?" Sighing hard, I withdrew and stuffed my wet cock into my dark grey slacks and zipped up. "Who the hell is making house calls at seven p.m. on a Sunday?" I rolled my eyes as I helped Tess up and wrapped her in her dressing gown. "It's not my asshat of a friend Frederick, is it? If it is, tell him I'm about to play with my wife and whatever nonsense he has to say, it can wait until tomorrow at the office."

"It's not Frederick," Suzette said quietly. "It's eh…I don't really know how to say this, Q, but…it's your brother."

CHAPTER TWO

BROTHER?
I didn't have a fucking brother.
I was an only child.
Well, only *legitimate* child.
My raping cunt of a father sired many others, with many other women who weren't my alcoholic mother. Other kids who I'd found hidden in a room attached to the stable block tucked in the estate's sprawling gardens. Kids ranging from infants to almost teens. All of them scared into silence and beaten into obedience. Their short lives used as a leash to control the unwilling harem my father kept in his bed.

Tess chased me down the stairs, her hands securing her dressing gown, hiding her nakedness. Rounding on her at the bottom, I snarled, "No way is another man seeing you in that scrap of a gown. I can see your nipples, *esclave*."

"Don't get all territorial. It's your cum trickling down my leg, no one else's."

My heart kicked. "And let's keep it that way. Go." I pointed back up the stairs. "Go and change. Give me ten minutes. I want to speak to him alone."

Her eyes flashed with familiar grey-blue fire.

Catching her around the nape, I breathed into her ear, "And don't rinse my cum away. I want you sticky and used. I want you to stay in that state until I have you again tonight."

Her lips twitched as she bowed her head, then flew back the way she'd come.

I had to readjust my cock again.

Damn woman.

Suzette skirted past me, heading to Franco's awaiting arm. He hugged her and shrugged at me. "What's going on?" he asked quietly.

I raised an eyebrow. "Who the fuck knows. Extortion? A threat? If he thinks he can milk me for money, he's going to find out it's a very bad idea to mess with me."

"He's in the library," Suzette said, keeping her voice down. "When I first opened the door, I swear I was looking at a younger version of you, Q, but…different too. I knew he had your blood even before he told me who he was."

"And who is he?" I raked a hand through my short dark hair, doing my best to stop thinking about Tess and my cum leaking down her leg.

"His name is Henri Ward."

"Nationality?"

Where did this little bastard end up when I'd shot my father and freed all his slaves? I'd done my best to give each woman a substantial fortune to live off after a lifetime of horror. And for those women with rape-begotten children, I'd forged any document they asked for, then flew them to whatever country they wanted to build a new life in.

Over the years, I'd kept tabs on them. I'd ensured they'd found some semblance of a happy existence. A few had died. A few lived on. And a few had obviously told their illegitimate offspring about their true origins, even though that'd been my one condition.

I would protect them financially.

I would atone for what my father had done to them but...under no circumstances were they to tell their children about me or my family.

I had enough shit to deal with without impromptu sibling reunions.

"He has an English accent, but he spoke French to me," Suzette replied.

"Age?" I shot a look at the closed doors to the library. The glass wasn't opaqued and I could see a shadow of someone standing by the limited edition leather bound classics by the fireplace.

"I'm guessing late twenties? Maybe a bit younger?"

Fuck.

He would've been one of the older ones in my father's stable then.

Did he remember living here?

Did he remember me marching into the midst of them, covered in patriarchal blood, gun in hand, and leading a trail of broken women to claim their bastards?

My hand shook a little as I shoved it into my pocket and spun on my heel. Tess appeared at the top of the stairs. The same stairs I'd stood on when Franco pushed her over my doorstep and commanded her to kneel before me.

She'd refused then and she'd refused me ever since.

Pity for both of us, her refusals got me hard and her wet and we'd become a match made in fucked-up heaven.

"You." I pointed a finger at her. "Stay there. I need to do this on my own." My eyes narrowed and I added a tad more gently, like a doting lover should, "We'll finish our conversation after."

Her lips quirked. "Conversation, huh? Very well, I very much look forward to *conversing* with you, husband."

My palm itched to remind her of her place all while I fought the lust and darkly tangled love she always drowned me in. "Behave and obey, Tess. Don't interrupt."

Stalking to the library, I wrenched open the double

doors, and came face-to-face with my half-brother.

One of many.

Hopefully, the only one who would ever know of my existence.

He was tall.

Maybe a shade taller than me.

Broad shouldered and lean waisted, with the type of physique that said he'd been in a few fights in his time and won.

He spun around as I closed the doors behind me and flicked the switch for privacy. The glass instantly went dark, blocking my nosy wife's eyes, giving me time to assess this new threat.

Because he was a threat.

A big one.

Motherfucking huge.

I'd chosen my family.

I didn't want any more springing from the shadows.

Especially ones with my father's blood running in their veins.

I had firsthand knowledge of that curse.

The Mercer Curse that'd been passed down by a man who raped, mutilated, and abused. I wouldn't will it on anyone. And I had every intention of avoiding all those who shared it because chances were very fucking high that I'd have to kill them for the very reasons I strived to deserve to live.

I hunted monsters.

I killed paedophiles and tore out the hearts of traffickers.

I made others hurt, all while the one person who should hurt the most was me.

The moment our gazes locked, he froze.

Grey eyes.

Stern mouth.

Stare of a beast.

He shared my unfortunate sharp widow's peak, same short dark hair, same five o'clock shadow that refused to be tamed by a razor, no matter how many times I shaved.

His jaw he'd inherited from our sadistic father, his cheekbones from an unfamiliar slave. His brows furrowed, casting his eyes in deeper shadows. His fists curled, matching mine, sensing my unwelcome without saying a word.

Neither of us spoke for the longest moment. Both assessing. Both forming conclusions on faces alone.

Finally, he said, "*Elle disait la verité.*" (She was telling the truth.)

I stiffened. Who was telling the truth? His mother? Some woman I'd done my best to protect, even at a personal cost?

"*Je suis désolé.*" (I'm sorry.) He tipped his chin, fighting for social etiquette. "*Je suis désolé de faire irruption comme ça mais... je n'avais pas le choix.*" (I'm sorry to barge in like this but...I didn't have a choice.)

Suzette was right. His French was impeccable, but the faintest English accent lurked beneath. Which slave was he whelped to? Which one broke her promise and told him about me?

A headache bloomed in my temples as I tried to recall the numerous women my father kept. Some from Asia, some from Europe, others from far off continents. There'd been a couple from the United Kingdom but not many.

Prowling forward, I did my best to keep my voice civil. "You may speak in English."

"Okay..." He never took his eyes off me as I chose one of the matching wingbacks and sat stiffly. Copying me, he took the other chair, our bodies facing one another, the empty fireplace full of shadows. "I, eh...there's no easy way to say this so—"

"You're the son of a slave. She told you about your origins and that my father was the cunt who created you. Am I correct?"

He stiffened. Clearing his throat, he nodded once. "That's about the gist of it."

"And why did you think you'd be welcome here?"

His eyes narrowed. "Because we're blood. Because I wanted to meet my—"

"We are not brothers. We merely share the unfortunate disease of similar DNA."

"It's because of that DNA that I'm here."

"In a place where you're not wanted."

Temper flared over his face. "Look, all I'm after is—"

"Money?"

His shoulders swooped back as if I'd offended him. "No. Fuck. Is that what you think? That I've come here with my hand out?"

"Didn't you? You must've researched me. You must know who I am if you've been clever enough to find my personal address."

The faintest tinge of embarrassment covered his cheeks. "I'll admit, I did spend a fair deal of time learning what I could about you."

I went deathly still. "And…what did you find out?"

He studied my coiled muscles. He read my body language correctly: understanding I was moments away from snapping and throwing him out of my home.

Would he run or would he fight?

Leaning back in the chair, doing his best to project calm, he said, "You're successful. Beyond successful. Your company is worth billions. You own real estate globally. On paper, you're nothing more than a bigshot corporate bastard who's probably done his fair share of dodgy dealings but…"

"But?" I snarled.

"I also found a few articles on your wife. The interview you both gave of how she came into your life. A slave you fell in love with. A girl who returned to you even when you freed her."

Fuck.

That article had been Tess's idea and one I'd spent a fuck-ton of money suppressing ever since. My role in slaughtering traffickers relied on them being confused on who I truly was.

Sure, it didn't hurt for them to see things online stating me as a wholesome family man. Someone trying to do the right thing. If anything, it helped form the persona that I was a straying son of a bitch who liked to keep broken women and cheat on his meek little wife, but I would prefer not to have criminals think the way to ruin me was to take Tess.

That'd already happened.

It'd almost killed me finding and saving her.

The heart of the man who took her still rotted beneath a rose bush outside.

And despite all my efforts to find her, fix her, and love her the way she needed me to love her, she'd shut down, shut me out, and put me through absolute fucking hell.

I traced one of the faint silver scars on my face from when she'd whipped me. A whipping that'd taken all my strength to endure but it had brought her back to me.

I'd chosen love over loneliness and some dark part of my heart nudged me to listen to this man.

I knew what it was like to hit rock bottom.

To feel so alone that death lured like a welcome utopia.

Forcing myself to relax a little, I softened my snarl. "Seeing as you know so much about me...let's talk about you." Steepling my fingers and resting my elbows on the wingback arms, I looked him up and down. "Henri Ward. Is that your real name? Where are you from? Why are you here? Tell me in as few words as possible why I should tolerate you in my home and why I should trust a thing out of your mouth."

Silence fell as he shifted uncomfortably. His lips twisted as if he chewed on words and discarded them before selecting a few and saying, "My name truly is Henri Ward but that surname was one my mother randomly created, not her true one. I can't tell you what that is because I don't know myself. All I'm asking for is...can I have your vow that you'll listen with no judgement? The whole journey here I promised myself I wouldn't do this.

That I'd follow the usual expectations of conversation between strangers, even if those strangers share blood. I wasn't going to blurt out my life story or every sordid mistake I've ever made. I mean...who does that? Who barges into someone else's house and vomits up their worst confessions? But..." He shrugged. "If I can't be honest with my brother, then who can I be? Chances are you won't want a thing to do with me anyway, so what have I lost by speaking the truth for the first time in my godforsaken life? I can't tell a therapist. I can't tell a friend. I definitely can't tell a lover. I've got no one else and...well, that makes you uniquely qualified for me to—"

"Get on with it," I snapped. "I despise ramblers."

He hung his head. "Rambling? Christ, I'm trying to be honest for the first time in my life. I need...fuck, I need..." He sighed and looked at the floor. "I-I tried to kill myself last month."

I sucked in a breath, shooting a glance at the library doors to make sure Tess stayed away like a good *esclave*.

"Go on," I said quietly.

He didn't look up, preferring to keep his eyes on the swirling, rich patterns of the carpet. "I'm...I'm sick." He growled under his breath. "No, that's wrong. I'm diseased. Not physically but spiritually. There's something broken inside me. I've felt it ever since I hit puberty...fuck." He laughed coldly. "That's a lie. I've felt it for far longer than that. Even when I was a boy, I felt different whenever I'd see violence in a movie or watch lovers have a quarrel in public. I'd get hot and tight, and I didn't understand what the crawling, gnawing sensation was until I had my first wet dream."

I waited for him to gather his thoughts, not making it any easier on him. I might not care what he had to say, but I gave him the quietness he needed to spill his confessions.

"I dreamed of blood," he breathed.

It was my turn to stiffen.

His story so far sounded eerily close to mine.

"I dreamed of fucking a girl and hurting her." He winced.

"I woke and found my sheets a mess. And ever since that day, I can't get those fantasies out of my head. I hid from them for as long as I could. I had a girlfriend in high school—for a couple of weeks at least. But she dumped my ass when she got sick of my lack of interest. I'd burn in shame whenever she'd reach for me because her innocent, gentle hand only made me soft." He wiped his mouth. "There I was, a fifteen-year-old guy, and I couldn't get it up. But whenever I'd break my self-control and watch porn late at night, I'd get hard as a fucking rock."

"What sort of porn?" I asked, surprisingly unshocked at his forthcomingness.

He didn't raise his eyes. "I can't believe I'm telling you this stuff. I've lost it. What the hell am I doing—"

"Keep going." I crossed my arms. "I'm listening."

He flinched and didn't reply.

I stayed quiet, letting the temptation to unburden himself outweigh social niceties. Finally, he cleared his throat and muttered, "I'd watch bad stuff. Choking. Breath play. BDSM but…not the role-play kind. The real kind where the tears are real, the pain is real, the blood is…real."

I unwound my arms and gripped my knees. I reneged on what I'd just said. "You're right. I have no idea why you're telling me this. No one in their right mind would come to a stranger's house and confess all the nasty shit inside them."

His grey eyes met mine, swimming in troubles and begging for salvation. "I-I have nowhere else to go. My mother….she, eh—" He cleared his throat. "She'd been ill for most of my life. Recurring breast cancer with periods of remission. It finally claimed her last month. I gave up my attempts at trying to be normal—working a dead-end job and pretending to fit in—and dedicated myself to being her caregiver for the past four months. She, eh, told me things…toward the end. She told me who my father was."

Ah, so it was a deathbed confession.

Something that'd eaten her alive and now she'd passed that demon onto her only son.

Stupid woman.

Why couldn't she have let that filth die with her?

She'd only condemned her son to a worser fate.

"Is that why you tried to kill yourself?" I asked clinically, feeling no emotion to the thought of him alive or in a grave.

"No. I mean…it was the slippery slope that led to it but no. You have to understand, I loved my mother. She was my only family but…she never seemed to love me in return. I've grown up forever trying to apologise for something I didn't understand. I always felt like I'd done something wrong and, until she told me the truth about my father and not the scripted lie that some asshole got her pregnant then ran off, I always felt like she blamed me for something."

"Blamed you how?"

He shrugged. "For living in a country that wasn't hers? For keeping her away from her parents and whatever extended family she had?" Sighing heavily, Henri added, "Whenever I'd ask why I didn't have grandparents to visit or cousins to play with she'd change the subject and say it was just us." Raking his hands through his short hair, he caught my eyes. "Just us was lonely. But now it's just me? It's fucking excruciating."

I would never admit that I knew exactly how crippling loneliness could be.

Clearing my throat, I asked briskly, "Do you have any idea where the rest of her family are? Go grace them with a visit instead of me."

He dropped his grey stare. "There wasn't a shred of information or paperwork in my mother's estate to hint where she's from. Not a single name. Not a whiff of an address. I have a feeling she might have been French Canadian, so perhaps I have relations there. She raised me bilingual—French and English. She also taught me Spanish but never told me why, or how she knew it."

Clasping his hands together, he added quietly, "And…if

I'm honest, I don't think—even if I could find a name or an address—that I'd approach any of her kin, not after she hid me away for so long. She kept me hidden for a reason. She didn't want me. I reminded her of something she'd rather not recall. It makes sense now I know the truth, but I think the shame and pain of my existence is something she happily died with, protecting her true family from ever knowing what happened to her and how I came to be."

I frowned, drawn in despite myself. "So you're saying you were brought up by a woman who didn't love you. That you put your life on hold to nurse her and when she died, you tried to commit suicide?"

He flashed me a tight smile. "Sounds pathetic when you say it like that. It makes me sound like some poor little boy who can't survive without his mother." Sighing heavily, he pinched the bridge of his nose. "The thing is…with her gone, I don't seem to have the strength to suppress the parts of myself that I've always fought. They're getting worse. The needs are getting worse. *I'm* getting worse. It's as if being utterly alone has allowed the darkness to consume me."

Ah, shit.

That wasn't good news.

I could see where this was going.

Where I'd gone.

Why I'd forbidden myself from touching a woman unless it was a paid professional, until Tess tripped into my heart. Why I'd murdered my father in cold blood and spent my entire life repenting for what he'd done.

I couldn't cure myself.

Couldn't turn off the blackness inside me.

I could merely live within the cage Tess kept me content in, ever so fucking grateful that she could withstand my violence, my sickness, my curse.

"You killed a girl?" I kept my voice deliberately calm. "You gave into that darkness?"

His answer would determine on him walking out of here alive or dying right there in the wingback.

He caught my gaze, flinching at whatever he saw in me. "No, I didn't go that far. But...I did hurt her. I was the idiot who got drunk and took a one-night stand back to my family home. The same home where I'd nursed my sick mother for the last four months. The home where I'd grown up in, always feeling unwanted. The home where my equally drunk partner asked me to 'play rough.'"

He cleared his throat and ran a shaking hand over his mouth. "I-I went too far. I didn't have any power against the needs inside me and...I spilled her blood on my childhood bedroom floor."

My hands balled. My gut churned. My mouth watered to end him.

"And you're here for me to bail you out? To get you off a criminal charge?"

"No." He slouched into the chair as if he wanted all his sins to devour him. "I'm not in that sort of trouble. But I also know what I did. I know how badly I fucked up. But I *did* stop. I stopped by turning that blackness on myself. I-I would've finished the job and put myself out of my misery if she hadn't taken the knife off me. She...forgave me. I compensated her. And...she left."

I stayed silent, letting him stew in his guilt.

Licking his bottom lip, Henri took his time forming his next sentence. "I came here because...I have nowhere else to go. No one else to call my own. I don't know how much longer I can keep fighting and I'm tired. I'm tired of being so fucking lonely all the time. I'm tired of being on my own. I'm tired of being *different*. So...I made a bargain with myself."

"A bargain?" I asked softly. "What sort of bargain?"

He didn't look up. "One that will either save me or condemn me. When I dug that blade into my thigh, hunting for a way to end it, I remembered what my mother said. That she'd been taken and raped for over a decade. That she'd birthed me in some chateau in France. That she'd done her best to raise me when she was granted the permission to spend time with me."

I studied him.

Did he remember that time?

Did he remember me?

His eyes locked on mine, answering my unspoken question. "I thought I'd recall something from my childhood driving up here. I thought for sure I'd recognise you if what she said is true. How could I have spent the first eight years of my life in a place I can't remember? How could I have a half-brother that I've never met? How could I have this disease inside me and have no way to get rid of it?"

I knew how.

I'd seen it happen in numerous slaves I'd rescued and rehabilitated.

Selective amnesia.

Deliberate blank spots in a traumatised psyche to exist the best it could.

For all his confessions, that one told me the most about Henri.

He was broken.

In motherfucking pieces and, in all honesty, those sort of fractures weren't fixable.

I knew from experience.

I'd clawed my way through my late teens and most of my twenties alone. Hiding who I truly was, drowning beneath nightmarish urges, begging the blackness in my soul to stop.

I was well acquainted with the allure of peace whispering on the promises of suicide. I knew how such offers of quietness and contentment could seduce.

I'd contemplated it a few times.

But each time I sank into such self-pity, I threw myself deeper into my work. I saved more slaves. I rescued those that'd been hurt by men like me. I did my best to erase my shame by giving back those lives that were ruined because of bastards that deserved to be dead.

But…we were at different stages of our war.

I fought mine on a daily basis and ensured I won every single night.

I was seasoned at this battle but Henri…

He's only just begun.

And that made him my enemy because it took every fucking shred to stay human, each and every day, and Henri already housed the beast. It'd sunk its fangs into him and no matter how much he thought he was winning, he wasn't.

It's only a matter of time.

Not *if* but *when* he killed someone.

And…I can't let that happen.

I shifted on my wingback.

A gun was hidden in one of the leather-bound editions across the library. All it would take was a silenced little pop and Henri could have the peace he deserved, and I could ensure he didn't hurt anyone else.

I went to stand.

Henri muttered, "My bargain to myself was…I'd ask for help before it was too late. From the only person I have left. So…I'm asking you. Brother to brother, stranger to stranger…c-can you help me?"

My legs refused to move.

Henri never looked away.

The imploring desperation in him made my hardened heart kick. I shut down any empathy I had toward him. I nodded, eyeing up the book that housed my murder weapon. "I'll help by—"

"Q?" The double doors cracked open as Tess stuck her head in. "Is everything okay?"

Fuck, not now.

She always did have the worst fucking timing.

Always messing with my plans by making me fall in love

with her and proving I wasn't so unredeemable, after all.

My eyes narrowed on my delectable wife. "Not now, Tess."

"But—"

"I said…*not now.*"

Her eyes fought mine. I had no doubt I'd get a tongue-lashing later, but I didn't want her hearing this. Seeing this. Not because she couldn't tolerate the darkness Henri spoke about but because she'd cajole me into letting him stay.

She'd force me to welcome him into the family.

She'd command me to give him somewhere safe.

She'd do that because…he was me.

This fucking stranger was *me*.

And it twisted me up in ways I didn't want to acknowledge.

I want him gone.

Now.

"I'll be out in a minute, Tess. Go."

Clenching her teeth, she paused for a moment then obediently drew the doors closed, leaving us alone again.

Sighing, I looked at my half-sibling. Perhaps killing him would be an overreaction. Eviction would have to do. "Look, I'm sorry for your loss and for everything you're dealing with, but you wasted a trip coming here. It's time for you to leave—"

"Wait!" Henri shot to his feet, towering over me where I sat. His black shirt and jeans sucked up the light in the room like a dead star.

Ever so slowly, calculatingly, I stood until our eyes were in line, our hearts at the same height. "Don't *ever* think you can command me in my own home, *boy*."

"Boy? I'm only eight years younger than you."

"Just because you saw my date of birth online doesn't mean—"

"I know because my mother told me you were sixteen when you shot your father. That you freed them. That you did everything you could to get them home to their own families."

I froze.

Fuck, how much had this woman told him?

Henri stepped into me, our chests almost touching. "Don't send me away. I'm not here for your money. I know you can't cure me. I know you'd probably rather kill me than accept me. And I know you have no reason to trust me but...I need to belong *somewhere*. I need...someone. Just a single person to hold me accountable. To keep me human."

Taking a step back, he tried to tame the urgency in him but failed. "I don't even know what I'm asking for just...I can't go back. I can't keep doing this—living like this. My own mother hated me. My own brother can't stand me. I've tried to be good. I obey the rules. I pretend to be like others. I do whatever it takes to fit in but...I'm done. I don't have the strength to dream such sickening things anymore. I barely exist because I'm fucking petrified I'm going to slip and hurt someone. I hate myself. I hate what I am, and I hate that I'm so fucking *alone*."

Breathing hard, he went to the fireplace and ran a finger over one of the very few pictures of Tess and me. It'd been taken outside in full summer with the sun shining and Tess sprawled over my front and me on my back. We'd both fallen asleep because the night before I'd proposed to her, put my ring on her finger, and then seared my brand into her flesh.

She'd branded me in return.

We'd fucked like absolute deviants.

And then, we'd passed out like teenagers on the lawn.

I smothered my snarl as he ran his finger over Tess's perfect face. Hanging his head, he murmured, "I-I want what you have. I came here to ask if you suffer the way I do. If you fight every damn day not to hurt those you desire but...I don't need to ask. I know."

Turning to face me, he shrugged. "I saw it in the way you spoke to her. The way you looked at her. The way she looked at you. You walk a fine line of disrespect and devotion and I...I want that. I *need* that. I want someone to call my own so I can stay a man, not a monster."

I bared my teeth, protective instincts surging through me. If he knew who else existed in this house—a beloved son I'd killed for many times over—he wouldn't be so quick to ask such fantastical things of me. "You think I can snap my fingers and conjure you a wife?" I laughed coldly. "You'd be better off asking me for money."

Crossing his arms, all his grief and loneliness vanished beneath a mask of ferocity.

It was like looking in a fucking mirror.

I hated it.

"I don't want money and I don't expect you to find me a wife. Despite everything I want, I know I'll most likely never be blessed in that way. I'll exist alone and I'll die alone but…in the small window of time I have left, I would very much like to know what it feels like to belong, even if it's to someone who can't stand me." He chuckled blackly. "After all, I'm used to that."

"Belong to what exactly?" I crossed my arms, matching him. "What's that supposed to mean?"

"It means I want my brother. I want at least one person to know who I truly am without being afraid of getting arrested for being honest—"

"I'd do worst than just arrest you." My eyes flickered to my hidden gun. "If you'd killed that girl, you wouldn't be breathing right now."

He froze. He studied me to see if I lied. When he found no such evidence, he braced his shoulders. "So…you didn't just stop murdering with our father? You kill other men like him? Other men like…us?"

Jesus Christ, how did he jump to that conclusion so quickly and why did I like it?

Why did my interest in him creep from intolerance to mild curiosity?

"I'd be careful if I were you." I stalked around the

library, moving toward the window. The very window where Tess had made me swear a blood oath to try loving her. She'd returned to me after I'd set her free. She'd become my air, my reason, my gravity and—

"Q?" The doors banged wide. "I'm sorry, but I really must interrupt." The object of my affection and annoyance came bounding into the library, heading straight toward Henri.

I pinched the bridge of my nose. "Fucking hell, Tess. You try my patience."

She flipped me the bird as she stopped in front of my unknown brother. She gasped as she studied his face. I growled as she cupped his cheek and traced his cheekbones that weren't mine on a face that clearly shared my genes.

Henri didn't say a damn word, shocked into silence, blinking as if an angel touched him.

Primal possession roared through me. "*Esclave, enlève tes mains de lui.*" (Get your hands off him).

Spinning to face me, she didn't flinch as I crossed the room and grabbed her wrist, tugging her away from Henri.

Her eyes widened, brimming with joy. "Oh my God, it's real. He's really related to you." She looked back at Henri. "I-I have no idea how this is possible—"

"It's possible because my father was a raping bastard who sowed seeds that shouldn't be sowed. You've met him and now he's leaving. Say goodbye—"

"Goodbye?" Her nose wrinkled. "But he just got here."

"And now he's going."

"But—"

"Say *au revoir*, Tess."

"Please…" Henri was wise enough not to come near us but the smile he shot my wife almost made me strangle him. "It's an honour to meet my sister-in-law."

"Nothing about her is yours," I snarled. "It's time you left—"

"Will you think on my request at least?" Henri asked. "It would mean—"

"What request?" Tess interrupted, pulling her wrist from my pinching hold. "I deserve to know. You're family." She elbowed me in the side. "He's family, Q. He's your brother."

"Half-brother." I scowled, rubbing where her sharp little appendage caught me.

"He's still blood."

"Yes, and he likes to *spill* blood," I hissed.

Her eyebrows raised. "As do you if I'm not mistaken."

Henri sucked in a breath.

I groaned. "*Esclave*, you're really not—"

"*Esclave*?" Henri scowled. "You call your wife *slave*? What the fuck?"

Tess grinned. "Think of it as sweetheart or darling. I always knew, even from the very first moment he called me that, that he was madly in love with me."

"Madly obsessed with you more like," I muttered. "Dangerously possessed. There's a difference."

"Not for us there isn't." She winked. "And we all lived happily ever after, even with your fetishes."

Goddammit, this woman.

Pressing a kiss to my cheek, she waved between me and Henri. "So...what's the story? You've been in here ages and are still glowering daggers at each other. Let's go get a drink. Have some dinner. Mrs Sucre is getting mighty tetchy that her soufflé is ruined because we didn't eat it in time."

"Tess, *mon amour*." I gritted my teeth. "Please leave. I'll escort Henri out and—"

"Dinner would be great," Henri interrupted, throwing a hesitant smile at Tess. "If it wouldn't be too much trouble?"

"Trouble? Oh no, Mrs Sucre always cooks far too much. You can meet Suzette and Franco and—"

"He's not staying, Tess." I did my best to hold on to my temper, failing by the second.

"Why not?"

"Because he's not welcome here."

"So that's what this is about?" Tess asked, flicking both of us a look. "Henri came looking for family and you're refusing to give him one? How can you not welcome your own flesh and blood, Q?"

Fucking woman.

She'd always read me too easily.

Always stuck her nose in where it didn't belong.

Before I could form an answer, Henri murmured, "I don't know a thing about either of you and you don't know a thing about me, but...I feel more myself in the twenty minutes I've been here than I have in my entire life. I feel like I can breathe. Like I'm...free. Not fully. I doubt I'll ever know what true freedom feels like, but I do feel as if I can relax a little. Like I won't fuck everything up by saying the wrong thing or admitting who I truly am." His grey eyes landed on mine. "If I can have that freedom for a few more hours before I'm evicted from your lives, then—"

"Nonsense." Tess smiled kindly. "You're my brother-in-law—"

"He's nothing to you, Tess. Just like you are nothing to him," I snapped.

"Jeez, stop being such a monster, *maître*."

Everything inside me went still, dark and dangerous. "Careful, *esclave*."

She drew herself up but didn't back down. "He came for you, Q. Don't you see? He needs you."

Henri wisely stayed silent.

I tripped into Tess's beguiling blue-grey eyes.

I could never refuse her anything when she got stroppy like this. Fiery and fierce and tempting my palm to bring her back into line all while she made me fucking beg.

"What do you need from him to prove he's looking for nothing more than company?" Tess crossed her arms.

At least she'd changed into a faint blue jumper and jeans.

She looked young and innocent, belying the temptress beneath. The temptress that'd turned me inside out and back to front all because she could handle the filth inside me.

An idea sparked.

An idea I tried to crush but couldn't.

She called me a monster?

I didn't like that label, but it fit.

It had always fit.

I *was* a monster.

To my enemies and my loved ones.

The curse never lifted.

The needs never faded.

I'd learned to exist despite them.

I was happy in *spite* of them.

But I remembered all too well the haunting, harrowing existence I'd lived before Tess came along. The agony of wanting what I couldn't have. The despicable need burning me up. The lust that came with so much disgust and shame.

If Henri fought such battles, I wasn't surprised he'd dabbled with the idea of ending it.

Wiping my mouth, I shook my head a little.

The idea kept evolving, spreading, unfolding like a map before me.

He could be useful.

He could be my secret weapon to infiltrate the clubs that knew who I truly was: the traffickers I'd dealt with in the past and managed to slaughter, only for new ones to spring up like weeds, fully aware of what I did and always one step ahead of my usual methods to hunt them down.

Lowering my hand, I studied Henri with new eyes.

Would he have the strength?

Would he lose his rotten soul if I threw him into the darkness where we both belonged?

"What are you thinking, Q?" Tess asked quietly. "I know that look and it's not good."

Ignoring my meddling little wife, I locked gazes with my half-brother and said the words that would ultimately break him or save him. "You want to belong? You want a ready-made family that sees you and accepts you? Fine."

Henri sucked in a harsh breath. "Really? Fuck, I can't thank—"

"There's a club. It's called The Jewelry Box. It's run by a sadist called Victor Grand. I've been trying to bring him down for years. I don't know where his club is, but I do know he's trafficked hundreds, possibly thousands, of girls and boys through his doors. No one has ever been found. All of them lost without a trace. I can't touch him because I have no one to infiltrate his operation. His intelligence is clever and always seems to find a link between the mercenaries I send in and me. He's ruthless, calculating, and a dangerous son of a bitch."

"Q...don't say what I think you're about to say," Tess murmured. "Please?"

"I will welcome you with open arms, *brother*." I smiled coldly. "All you have to do is prove yourself."

"Prove myself?" Henri asked, equally as coldly. "Prove myself how?"

"Go to Paris. Befriend whoever you need to befriend to get an invitation into The Jewelry Box. I'll put a tracker on you and, if you're welcomed into this sordid, sickening world, you will lead me right to his estate and will help me exterminate him, once and for all."

"You want me to infiltrate a sex ring?" Henri's face went white. "I've just told you why I can't be around that sort of thing. Why I'm here instead of in a ditch somewhere. I-I wouldn't be able to survive the temptation."

I shrugged. "That's your problem, not mine. You asked to be accepted. I'm saying I'll accept you, but only if you prove that you're like me. That you suffer the same desires, drown beneath the same darkness, yet you're strong enough to stay in the light. It takes monumental strength to survive the curse we've been given. And if you're too weak, then...I want nothing to do with you."

Wrapping my arm around Tess, I led her toward the exit. Before heading into the foyer and the dining room beyond, I turned to look back at Henri. "You can think it over tonight. You can have dinner with us. I'll give you a bed. I'll tolerate your presence. But until you prove that you aren't like our father—that you won't give in and become him. That you're better than all the evil swimming in our veins...you won't be permitted to stay or belong."

Henri raked a hand through his short hair. "And if I don't? If I refuse to infiltrate this club? If I know in myself that I'll fail? What then?"

"You've just shared your darkest secrets. You made the choice to come to a stranger's house and divulge things that honestly makes me want to kill you. I see what you are. I see you're telling the truth. And really...the kindest thing I can offer you is a bullet. But...you get one chance. One chance to prove you have the desire to stay good. If you do, then you've bought yourself some time to earn my trust. But if you don't do what I ask...if you don't agree to do whatever it takes to prove I shouldn't exterminate you, just like I exterminate them—if you fail at helping me destroy Victor and his Jewelry Box, if you fail to resist the temptation of broken slaves, if you fail at keeping your dick in your pants and your hands free from blood, then...so help you, *brother*, I will find you, I will hurt you, and you will wish you never set foot in my house, kin or no kin."

"You'd kill me?" Henri winced. "You'd kill me just because I'm sired by the same bastard who sired you?"

"I'd kill you because I know what you suffer. I know how close I've come to hurting others. Therefore, I know what you're capable of. I'd kill you to protect those innocents, but I'd also kill you to free you from the same pain that's driven me mad all my life."

He watched me warily. "And if I succeed?"

"Then you are worthy of the Mercer name, and you

will never be alone again."

Henri looked at Tess snuggled against my side and a look of such visceral longing, such heart-wrenching hope, twisted his strangely familiar face.

He'd managed to survive this long but it wasn't a life he'd been living.

It'd been a prison.

A carefully fortified jail to keep himself in check.

If he could prove he was better than our father, that he had the power to control himself, then I would teach him how to find joy even while being the worst kind of beast.

I never thought I'd have the urge to help another like me.

But…that was before.

This was now.

But so help me God, if he failed, his guts would be ribbons, his blood would be spilled, and his heart would join the other one rotting under my rose bush…

EPILOGUE

I FOUND TESS GIVING OUR SON, LINO, a goodnight kiss.

His bedroom reminded me of summer with clouds sketched on the ceiling and the bird stencils we'd painted on the walls flying with wild abandon.

I smiled and crossed my ankles, reclining against the door frame. The day Tess had announced Abelino was old enough to design his own room, we'd been covered in paint as much as the walls. I'd balanced our small son on my shoulders while Tess gave him a paint brush and held up the stencil of a flying duck, laughing as he half painted the wall and half painted my face.

"Mum?" Lino stretched in his comfy bed as Tess stroked his tussled brown hair. "Who was that man I heard at dinner? Why couldn't I come join you guys?" His sleepy, innocent voice made me tense on the threshold.

I'd asked Suzette to keep Lino far away from Henri.

She'd done what I asked, spending the night with our son and the chaos of dogs that always followed him. Dogs that I hadn't had a choice in adopting after Tess dumped them into my long-suffering heart.

"Just a friend, *mon coeur*." (My heart.) Tess kissed his forehead again. "Sorry for waking you. Go back to sleep."

"Is Courage still here?" He yawned. "I can't sleep without him."

The damn dog's ears pricked at his name. He leaped onto the bed, circling twice before sprawling over Lino's short legs.

The feral depth of love I had for my child threatened to cripple me.

He chuckled. "Good. Now I can go back to sleep." Spying me by the door, he waved. "*Nuit, Papa.* (Night, Dad.)

"*Bonne nuit, mon fils.*" (Goodnight, my son.) I bowed my head.

"Sweet dreams." Tucking him in, Tess sighed with unconditional affection then tiptoed to me and slipped beneath my arm.

My chest ached with overwhelming gratitude.

I was the luckiest son of a bitch in the whole goddamn world.

Silently, we walked down the long corridor toward the staircase at the end that led to our tower.

My inherited chateau had undergone many renovations since I'd claimed the keys. Its untold wealth and sordid history was carved into every keystone, but it'd never been more precious to me now it housed my wife and son.

Climbing the curling stone steps to our bedroom, I sighed with relief as we stepped into our playroom and sanctuary. The chains, where I'd strung Tess up the night I got drunk and shattered my self-control, waited, tucked and secretive, in the rafters. The chest full of toys and debauchery beckoned to be opened and played with.

Despite my promise of taking her again, the moon was almost setting, and I was fucking drained. Henri had been given one of the guest suites as far away from us as possible, yet I felt his invasion in every cell.

Tomorrow, I'd sort out a bank account with enough funds for him to buy his way into The Jewelry Box, ensure his online presence couldn't be traced back to me, and then...he was leaving and never coming back.

I hid my wince.

For all my promises of welcoming him if he proved himself, I already knew it would never happen. He was a dead man walking. By my hand, his, or someone else's. I refused to get attached to a beast that would be dead before the year was through.

Slipping out from beneath my arm, Tess padded toward our bed.

Pulling back the white coverlets and tossing a few of the nonsense pillows she said looked homely onto the floor, she asked, "You don't truly intend on sending him into a trafficking hellhole do you, Q?" Pausing with a beaded cushion in her hands, she pinned me with a condemning stare. "He'll last ten minutes."

I shrugged out of my blazer and draped it over the chaise. "He came here asking for something I'm not prepared to give, *esclave*. Until he proves himself, I don't care what happens to him."

"Then *help* him prove himself." She tossed the cushion to the carpet. "He's lost." Her voice turned quiet. "Watching him at dinner…the way he couldn't take his eyes off us whenever we touched. He's full of longing and loneliness. So much so, it's killing him."

"It's either that which kills him or something else."

Her eyes snapped to mine. "It doesn't have to end that way. He's going to do what you asked. You know he'll try. The determination with every question he asked tonight proves he's willing to do whatever it takes. You heard him. He's got nothing to lose. Nowhere to go. No one to care for."

"Then maybe he'll survive through sheer audacity."

I refused to give into her cajoling.

I'd let her force four dogs into my life by tugging expertly on my heart strings. I'd allowed her to work beside me while I rehabbed untold number of sex-slaves. I let her travel with me to exterminate the bastards that popped up like rabies-infected gophers. I had a son with her, despite my fear that one day he would turn out to be like me.

But I would *never* let her put herself in harm's way again.

It'd almost killed me losing her before.

I still had fucking nightmares at what they did to her and how I was almost too late.

The thought that those cunts could take my child too?

Fuck no.

Brother or no brother. Blood or no blood.

He meant nothing compared to Tess and Lino.

"You can increase his odds, you know." She hugged another cushion. "Train him. Teach him. Give him time to prepare—"

"There's no preparing for acting like a raping motherfucker. You either are one or you're not."

She stilled, hearing the truth in my callous tone. "And there it is." She shook her head and dropped the cushion, adding it to the graveyard of all the others. "You don't think he's redeemable. You think he's your father. And just like you killed your father, you're willing to kill your brother too."

"And any other sibling who comes asking for a home." I balled my hands. "I know what lives inside him, Tess." I thumped my chest. "I feel it every damn day, every fucking second. Right here. Deep, deep within. I've only lasted this long because I have you. He has no one. There's no fucking way he'll have the strength to fight those urges for much longer. I'm surprised he's lasted this long. We're at different stages of our sickness, *esclave*. I know what he's fighting, and I don't want him anywhere near my family. If by some miracle he's successful in infiltrating The Jewelry Box, he'll lose himself the moment he steps foot in there."

"Then why the hell did you ask him to do it?" she snapped.

Unbuttoning my shirt, I kicked off my shoes and padded in my socks to the bathroom. "Because I'm giving him what he asked for. He wanted something to care about. I've given it to him. Tomorrow, I'll set him up with enough funds so he can play the part of sadistic sociopath, ensure there are no loose ends that link him back to me so he'll be safe, and tag him with a tracker so

I can monitor his every move, but then he's leaving and never coming back."

Shit.

I hadn't meant to say that.

"Never coming back…? What do you mean, never coming back? Oh my God." Her eyes flew wide. "You're just using him as bait. You figure you can have him lead you to where Victor Grand's sex island is and then clean up the mess."

"It's late, Tess—"

"That's why you went into such detail at dinner. Why you spent an entire evening going over where Victor was last spotted hunting and the names of those in cahoots with him." Anger laced her words. "You know he'll do anything to get you to accept him and you're using that for your own gain."

"Not my own gain, wife. *Their* gain. All the slaves currently serving in that hellhole. I'm using him to free them."

"You could free him at the same time."

"There's no freeing a man like that." I tore off my shirt, revealing my heavily tattooed chest covered in sparrows. "There's no freeing a man like me."

She shook her head. "You *are* free. If you can be happy…he can too."

I sighed heavily and went to her. She swayed backward but didn't fight as I wrapped her in my arms. "I'm not free, *esclave*. I'm leashed and collared. I have faith in you to keep me in-line. *Je suis ton maître, mais tu es le maître de mon âme.*" (I am your master, but you are the master of my soul.)

Pressing a soft kiss on one of my inked feathers, she murmured into my chest, "Then help him find his own master. Someone who can leash and collar him too."

Resting my chin on her head, I let silence settle around us.

I didn't share my true thoughts with her.

I didn't admit that I had a suspicion I'd be the one who would end up killing him, in justice or in mercy.

I didn't confess that I hoped Henri took the money and was smart enough to run far, far away.

Maybe if he kept running from temptation, he would survive.

He didn't have to do this. He didn't have to be the broken hero.

But if he accepted my suicidal request—if he infiltrated The Jewelry Box and vanished into a world of sin—then the next time I saw him, I had no doubt blood would be spilled.

"Just promise me you'll do whatever it takes to help him, Q." Tess snuggled closer. "You know how ruthless these traffickers can be. How dangerous and wily they are. Just…be kind to him. Don't throw him to the wolves."

I sighed and pushed her away just enough to kiss her.

Her perfect taste slipped onto my tongue.

My heart pumped with overwhelming love.

When the kiss ended, I whispered, "But if I throw him to the wolves, perhaps he'll grow fangs and fight. Maybe he'll turn out to be the worst wolf of all and he won't need my help."

"Or he'll be shredded alive."

Taking her hand, I guided her to bed. "He's a Mercer, Tess. We might be cursed but…if he wants love as much as I did, then…who knows? Maybe he'll be strong enough to break that curse. Maybe I have him all wrong and he'll succeed. Maybe someone else will be strong enough to muzzle him. Maybe he'll destroy them or maybe he'll destroy himself, either way…destruction is what he needs."

"That poor man has no idea what he's just agreed to," she whispered sadly.

"That's his cross to bear, not ours." Stripping my wife, I undressed and crawled into bed with her.

As she slotted against me, skin to skin, bone to bone, I cradled her tight and made two promises.

One, I would do as Tess asked and be a little kinder toward him. If, by some miracle, he succeeded then…I would let him stay.

And two, if he failed…if he slipped into hell and drowned in the darkness that cursed us, I would put him out of his misery.

I would ensure he never saw death coming.

Because that was what brothers did.
We did what was necessary.
We did what was right.
And killing Henri Ward might be the only right thing to do.

Are you ready to read Henri's tale?!

RUBY TEARS (Book One of The Jewelry Box Series) *follows his descent into darkness, no matter how much he tries to abstain....*

Releasing throughout 2024.

*If you haven't met **Q & Tess** yet, their dark romance is complete and is available in Kindle Unlimited for a short time!*

Start with **TEARS OF TESS**

SNEAK PEEK INTO

Ruby Tears

PROLOGUE

TEN THOUSAND DOLLARS.
That pitiful sum changed my entire life.
It *bought* my entire life.
A measly ten thousand dollars, given to my boyfriend by a monster to fuck me.
He took it.
The monster took me.
And I never saw freedom again.

CHAPTER ONE

Henri

WHO THE FUCK WAS I kidding?
I can't do this.
I didn't have the morals, the self-control, the *strength*.
Even suggesting I try to do this was like dumping an oblivious goat into a T-Rex paddock. The goat thought he'd scored a good spot—a nice place for a snack and a snooze, only to end up decapitated and spat all over the foliage.
I honestly didn't know if I was the T-Rex or the goat in this scenario.
Honestly, I was both.
It took all my fucking willpower to restrain myself. To smother the parts of me that were rotten and monstrous all while doing my best to be good. To be a genuinely nice guy who didn't crave such debasement.
To be like *him*.
My half-brother who'd fought such urges and won. Who'd not only survived with the inherited compulsion to cause tears and get hard on pain but to also find a wife capable of leashing him.

Fuck, I wanted that.

I wanted the freedom to be me, all while too shit terrified to even approach a girl these days.

Not after what I'd done.

Not after what I'd wanted to *keep* doing.

The familiar black hunger clawed its way through me, and every despicable part of me came out to play. My hearing seemed to sharpen, my nose became more acute to the scents of writhing, sweaty bodies dancing in the club around me; even my teeth ached as if they could lengthen, ready to puncture sweet flesh and lap up the hot essence inside—

Christ, stop it.

Do you hear yourself, Ri?!

My fist spasmed around my glass of whiskey.

The cheap imitation crystal fractured, cracked, then exploded into shards, tearing through the meat of my palm and drenching my newly purchased suit in liquor.

"*Merde*, you okay, Ward?"

Ward.

The name on my falsified birth certificate but not my true name.

My true name I'd only just found out, and under no circumstances could it be uttered around this scum.

Cursing under my breath, I glanced at the man beside me.

The man I'd painstakingly stalked, befriended, and done whatever it took to gain his trust. Six months it'd taken. Six months to slime my way into his inner circle when I should've run in the opposite direction.

He was the type of human I did my utmost to avoid because he represented who I truly was at my core. Each time I hung out with him—slowly evolving from shared drinks with acquaintances to watching dark-web porn in his den—I came face to face with the monster inside me.

It clawed and snarled. It thirsted for things not normal. It howled for things not sane. My dreams were full of despicable deeds, and my body hardened at the foulest images. The first time

I'd been invited to his house to watch some sick shit he subscribed to, I'd had to run to the bathroom to throw up.

Just because I had urges didn't mean I would ever, fucking *ever*, give in.

I'd walked away when I'd wanted to keep going. I still had a shred of decency...unlike the animals in those movies.

But, little by little, video clip by video clip, I shut down the parts of me that I'd clung to all my life. I turned my back on the last embers of light and embraced the disturbing darkness within me.

That choice had gotten me this far.

But at what cost?

My fucking soul, that's what.

"Yeah, I'm fine," I muttered, snatching a serviette from the holder on the bar, watching with morbid satisfaction as the pristine white soaked a vibrant red with my blood.

I shuddered as I imagined someone else's blood. A nameless woman with her eyes wet and legs spread—

Fuck.

Clenching my teeth, I scrubbed at the wound.

I was so fucking twisted.

I should've just killed myself when I had the chance—done myself a favour instead of being weak and reaching out to my half-brother. A sibling I hadn't even known existed until my mother told me on her deathbed four months ago. I'd thought my father was a deadbeat who'd knocked her up, then left her with nothing and no one.

Turned out, my origins were far, far worse.

"Looks deep, man." Roland grabbed my wrist and inspected my wound. My skin crawled where he touched me, but I kept a perfectly schooled grimace on my face. It would not help my case if he learned how many murdering fantasies I'd had since entering this nightclub with him.

He was lucky I hadn't grabbed the velvet rope stands of the queue outside and bludgeoned him around the head. Incredibly lucky I hadn't shoved a microphone down his throat from the awful singing DJ or smashed a bottle of expensive Johnnie Walker and stabbed his jugular with glass shards.

My nostrils flared as his fingers tightened around me, then fell away.

Keep it together, asshole.

I only had one chance at this.

One.

If I succeeded in doing what my half-brother demanded of me, I would have a family for the first time in my godforsaken life. But if I failed…that family I wanted so desperately would slit me from ear to ear and bury me in an unmarked grave. Probably with my heart torn out and cock ripped off, just like he'd promised.

"Ah, *merde*, he's here. Mop up that massacre." Roland chuckled, sending his baguette and chocolate éclair-loving guts jiggling. "Then again, he might like it. Maybe the Master Jeweler will make *you* bleed tonight instead of some poor girl."

I kept my lips plastered into a grin instead of reaching for the glass splinters on the ground and driving them into his eyes. For a man who indulged in sexual appetites as much as he, I wasn't sure how Roland hadn't burned off the layer of fat he carried.

He'd be such easy prey.

If everything went well, I would eventually have the pleasure of killing him.

Unless my half-brother killed me first.

Pressing the serviette a little harder against the still oozing cut, I looked up to where his watery blue eyes had focused. I'd befriended Roland Olivan the Third thanks to my half-brother informing me he was one of the last remaining bastards who dared dabble in forced pleasure in France.

My older bro had done a particularly good job of exterminating most of them but the odd one kept sprouting up like weeds, infected with the same curse I had. The same plague that was passed on by my father.

"Don't make me regret this, Henri." Roland hastily smoothed down his custom-made navy suit. The expensive material shimmered under the crystal ball twinkling above, painting him with wealth, even if his eyes remained that of a thief. A thief who stole lives for his own pleasure.

"How would I make you regret this?" I growled, stuffing the bloody serviette into my black suit pocket and ensuring my dull bronze tie was perfectly smooth. My gold cufflinks sparkled, making my heart thud.

The simple birdcage emblems seemed to shout who I truly was. That I was descended from the Mercer line and in cahoots with the infamous Q.

The cufflinks had been his idea.

Not because he'd wanted to welcome me to his family but because he didn't trust me.

The tracking device no doubt told him exactly where I was right now and where I'd end up if tonight was a success.

Supposed I should be grateful.

If tonight went well, I doubted I'd be in France much longer. If it all went to shit, perhaps Q could use the cufflinks to find and save me. Then again, he'd probably conclude I'd lost myself in the cesspit of sin and come kill me instead.

I had an awful feeling that was his plan all along.

He was seasoned at this. He knew how these trafficking bastards worked. He knew how slippery and evil they were. The fact he hadn't given me any training, no weapons, and not even a back-up plan told me everything I needed to know: he didn't care if I won or lost.

He probably wanted me to fail so he didn't have to welcome me into his home.

"Remember what we talked about?" Roland asked, looking me up and down with a critical sneer. "You like gemstones. You enjoy taking raw stones and breaking them apart to show the priceless rock within. Tell him how much you enjoy smashing those jewels and—"

"You expect me to speak in code all night?" I turned to face him, balling my hands and wincing at the fresh pain on my palm. The pain was good…helped me focus. The pain was bad…made me lose control. "Pretty sure he won't care if I speak plainly." I swallowed the sour taint on my tongue and let the beast within me wake. "I think he'd appreciate my honesty if I say how much I crave their screams. How I can't sleep at night, picturing how skin bruises and bleeds. How I have dreams of helpless conquests all begging me to stop. And I bet he'd welcome me with open arms if I confess that the moment they start to struggle, I get hard as a fucking rock—"

"It sounds as if you're listing my own fetishes, which is rather disconcerting, seeing as I've never met you before."

I froze.

The hair on the back of my neck prickled.

The monster inside me snarled to meet this other beast. To find kinship in shared sickness. But my struggling goodness did its best to remember this was a ruse.

I'd agreed to do this to prove I wasn't like them. Not to turn my soul over to the devil.

Fuck.

Sweat rolled down my spine as I slowly turned to face the Master Jeweler.

I did my best to smile like a human, but the moment the suave, self-composed asshole—who was rumoured to have singlehandedly trafficked over a thousand people—met my eyes, he knew.

He knew, just like my half-brother had known.

I might want to be good.

I might have fought all my life to remain a worthwhile citizen who pretended to be like everyone else, cared for his sickly mother, and paid his taxes on time, but the truth was…I wasn't.

I was a monster.

Just like this bastard.

And I officially signed my death warrant by shaking his hand and stepping willingly into his den.

CHAPTER TWO

Ily

"COME ON, Il, JUST ONE more drink."

I looked at the sparkling disco ball above and said a silent prayer to whoever would listen. *Please give me the strength not to break up with him. Not tonight. Tonight is his birthday. He's a spoiled little birthday boy who smudged my carefully applied makeup with a blowjob. A blowjob I wasn't all that keen on giving him, by the way—*

"Are you listening to me?" Sam waved his hand in front of my face. "Hellllooo. Dammit, Ily, you've got that spaced-out look in your eyes again."

Was it my fault that I found my own thoughts more entertaining these days?

How had we ended up like this?

Four years together and every day became more and more of a struggle. I'd had such high hopes that Paris would rekindle whatever spark we had. *But alas…I spent my final meagre pounds on a dream.*

"Jesus, woman. You gonna blink at me like a drunken owl all

night or open your mouth and say something?"

I snapped out of my thoughts, smacking my coral-painted lips together. "My mouth was plenty open back at the hotel. So open, in fact, you were able to put something inside it if I recall."

He sighed heavily, just like I knew he would. "It's my birthday. A blowjob is tradition."

"Not our tradition."

"Every year, you've given me one."

"By *choice*, Sam, not by force."

"*Force?*" His eyebrows shot up. The reddish-brown mop on his head glistened from the product he'd used to tame it off his high forehead. His green eyes glittered with anger. "I have never forced you. Not once."

"I said I was feeling queasy. That the pastrami from lunch wasn't sitting right. Yet you moaned and groaned and guilt-tripped me so badly that it was easier to drop to my knees and say '*ah!*' rather than keep arguing."

The anger in his eyes deepened. "You and I both know that your excuses when it comes to sex are getting more and more common." His voice rose a few octaves, supposedly imitating me. "Oh, not tonight, Sam, I've started my period. Oh sorry, didn't I tell you? I agreed to go out with Alicia tonight. Oh shit, I have to work late—"

"Working late is a legitimate reason to refuse—"

"Ever since you got that promotion, you've made it almost impossible for me to spread your legs." He pouted and crossed his arms. He looked like a petulant brat instead of a twenty-five-year-old pharmaceutical sales rep.

I honestly couldn't remember why I once believed I was in love with him. Once upon a time, I found his pale skin, faint freckles, and cultured upbringing a turn-on. When he'd walked into the Tower of London gift shop with his then girlfriend (a mousy girl who cringed from the meat-eating crows), I couldn't take my eyes off him.

Seemed the feeling was mutual because he'd come back the next day and the next, which didn't make any sense because he lived in London and had been force-fed England's morbid medieval history since the crib.

Turned out, *I* was the special attraction.

For a while, he'd been sweet and mostly doting but the past year, he'd hardened and turned a little cruel. His gaslighting had also gotten terribly out of control.

"I'm proud of that promotion." My chin tipped up like it always did when I got snippy. "It took years for them to notice me."

"You're a glorified office manager."

I didn't bother telling him how hard I worked for more responsibility. How most positions within the heavily fortified fortress were only given to the beefeaters and their kin. What I really wanted to do was work with the priceless crown jewels, but only three people in the entire world were allowed to touch them. Knowing I'd never put my gemmology qualification into use—unless I somehow became the queen—didn't make my dreams any less real.

"Ah, I see where this is going," Sam muttered, planting his hands on his hips like he always did when arguing with me. He believed it made him look important. I believed it made him look like an arrogant ass. "You're still hanging on to the idea that one day you'll be allowed to fondle their crowns and sceptres and whatever other diamond-encrusted baubles they have under lock and key."

"Can I help that I like pretty things?"

His nose wrinkled. I braced myself for another tirade, but he exhaled heavily and dropped his hands. "You're a pretty thing. Can I help that I like *you*?"

I stiffened, but accepted the olive branch for what it was. "Thank you for the compliment."

Smiling wider, doing his best to shed the tension between us, he slid his arms around my waist and pulled me closer. We stood on the outskirts of the busy dance floor and the noisy racket classified as dance music blared far too loudly. The fact that we'd been able to argue at all was a small miracle.

"I've always found you gorgeous. You know that." His hand skated up my side and played in the pin-straight, blue-black hair skimming my collarbones. Sam definitely had Irish somewhere in his lineage, but—if I believed the fairytales my adoptive father whispered to me—then I was the half-blooded descendant of a maharajah.

According to him, somewhere, somehow, a king had corrupted a maiden and created my family line. If I hadn't been dumped outside the local hospital where my father worked as a heart surgeon, I might never have existed past a few days old—bastard child of a long-ago maharajah or not.

Luckily, I now belonged to the best people in the world, and a pang of homesickness filled me.

We'd only been in Paris two nights, and I already wanted to leave.

I miss Krish. Wonder what he's doing right now?
Damn, this was a mistake.
This relationship.
This holiday.
I...I'm done.

I'd been done for months, yet it'd taken all my savings and a foreign country to finally admit that.

Sam brought me closer, his lips puckering to kiss me. His eyes closed in preparation for making out in a raucous French nightclub.

I braced myself.

I went to kiss him back.

Only...in the time it took for our lips to meet, a surge of bravery washed through me. The strange courage was definitely ill-advised, but I couldn't fight it anymore.

I couldn't stop the urge to flee and be free.

"Sam." I swayed back, refusing his kiss. "Sam...we need to talk."

His eyes flew wide, the glittery disco ball dancing in his green gaze. "What?" He cocked his head against the music. "What did you say?"

Great.
I finally get the strength to break it off, and he can't even hear me.
I could just pretend I hadn't said anything.
Pretend I was happy.
Pretend I was fine.
But...I needed out.
Right here.
Right now.
Tonight.

Taking his hand, I tugged him away from the writhing dance floor. If I was going to do this, we both needed a drink.

His fingers latched around mine as he followed me.

We weaved around a sea of dancing, happy people, ducked around a few bouncers, then reached the crowded bar.

Taking a gulp of air no longer tainted by smelly sweat, overpowering men's cologne, and overly sweet perfume, I tried to get the barkeep's attention.

"Hi!" I waved my hand as Sam plastered himself against me.

"Hey, over here." I waved harder, desperate for something to bolster my rapidly flagging courage.

"Getting in the mood, huh? I like it." Sam's hand slid down my ass, going far too deep and low. I flinched as his fingers probed between my legs, digging my flouncy rose gold skirt into my unmentionables.

My entire body jerked, not with passion or familiarity but with dreadfully building disgust.

Shifting my hips and doing my best to dislodge his fingers, I threw him a scowl. My lips parted to command he stop pawing me—

But...

Something farther along the bar.

Some*one.*

Someone who stopped my heart and made the awful music screech to silence in my ears.

Oh, dear lord in fanciful heaven.

Who.

The.
Hell.
Is.
That?

My gaze completely bypassed Sam and zeroed in on a demigod.

The man had to be descended from gods because no one, I meant *no one*, looked as impossibly perfect as he did.

Dark hair cropped close to his head. Lips a shade too red that only seemed to paint him with violence instead of seduction. Shadowed dark eyes and an impeccably shaven jaw. Cheeks that were slightly hollow and a throat clenching with power.

His lips thinned as he rolled them together, nodding at something his companion said.

His nose flared slightly as if he felt the same snap of awareness I did but couldn't understand why.

Slowly, his head tipped up.

His gaze scanned the pumping club, his entire body full of predatory calculation.

My tummy fluttered.

His tongue flicked out and ran over his bottom lip, searching.

Look over here.

I couldn't catch a proper breath.

I wanted him to see me. Just like I saw him. I wanted to know if he felt the same unexplainable flash of incinerating heat. A heat I'd never felt before, even in the hottest moment of passion.

His shoulders tensed as he kept looking.

My heart skipped twenty beats as it tried to remember how to work. My knees gave up being bone and became melted butter instead.

"What can I get you?" A woman leaned over the sticky bar and yelled in my ear.

All the music slammed back.

All the chaos and smells and…ill-advised courage.

Tearing my gaze from the demigod as he returned to

glowering at the man beside him, I locked eyes with the pretty bartender and yelled far too loudly, "I'm breaking up with my boyfriend, and we need shots."

Sam went rigid beside me.

The girl's brown eyebrows shot to her pixie haircut.

And I swayed on the spot as the demigod suddenly looked past his companion and locked gazes with me.

Grey.

His eyes are dark grey.

He froze like I had.

Froze as if he smelled me from there and decided in a single moment that he very much wanted to eat me alive.

I didn't know if I wanted to run away as fast as possible or offer myself up on a silver platter.

"What the fuck is going on, Ily?" Sam's fingers dug into my upper arms, spinning me to face him. My nape prickled, hating that I couldn't see the man who made my instincts sing with deep, dark warnings.

"You're breaking up with me?" His face contorted into something scary instead of English charm. "What. The. *Fuck?*"

The bartender placed a long wooden board next to us with six shots of amber liquor. I looked from Sam's rage to the shot.

I made the choice to administer some liquid courage.

Snatching two glasses, I tossed them back, winced at the fire, gasped, choked, coughed, coughed some more, then sucked in a wheezy breath.

"I know it's your birthday, Sam, but...I've given you a blowjob, so I think it's only fair that you give me a divorce."

CHAPTER THREE

Henri

MY EARS RANG, COMPLETELY DROWNING out what the Master Jeweler was saying.

Blowjob?

Divorce?

Who the hell was this girl, and why did her voice pierce through all the other noise in this godforsaken club, somehow hijacking my rotten heart? That same fucking heart tripped over its pathetic self the moment I caught her eyes. I couldn't tell what colour they were, but the disco ball above granted the illusion that they flickered with purples and blues.

I had a sudden urge to shove away all the people between me and the object of my dangerous fascination and demand to know who she was.

But that would be stupid.

Beyond fucking stupid.

And it wasn't her that caused my chest to seize or my perfectly pressed pants to grow unnervingly tight.

It was this.

This assignment.

This task—given to me by my half-brother who'd had years learning how to tame his tendencies—only to throw me into those same tendencies without any boundaries.

Another droplet of sweat ran down my back.

If I couldn't even handle standing here talking, how was I going to handle everything else?

"Ward?"

The Master Jeweler quirked a manicured dark blond eyebrow at me. Roland pressed his elbow into my side, ripping me back to the suave, despicable man currently watching me with questions in his knowing eyes. Ever so slowly, the Master Jeweler turned on the balls of his glossy shoes and peered at the girl who'd sent a bolt of sick electricity to my chest with a single glance.

Her hair hung heavy and straight, kissing her shoulders with an almost impossible shade of sapphire-black. It had to be fake. No one had hair like that.

I balled my hands as my gaze followed the Master Jeweler's, both of us studying the sweep of her shoulder blades—visible beneath the flimsy strings of her navy top—following the strong line of her spine (with the hint of a tattoo) down to the swell of her ass, hidden beneath a gold-pink skirt.

My throat closed as my gaze drifted lower, drinking in the long expanse of tanned legs, snagging on silver ankle boots with savagely sharp heels.

With a low chuckle, the Master Jeweler turned to face me, nodding appreciatively. "This club attracts sparkling gems. It's a great place to fill a jewelry box full of pretty things." His flat blue gaze snapped to Roland. "Don't you agree, Olivan?"

Roland gave him an oily smile. "Oh, definitely, *bijoutier*. I myself have been lucky enough to collect quite a few *bijoux* on my hunts here."

My ears perked on the French words for jeweler and jewels.

I was fluent from birth—thanks to my mother being half-French.

"Pourquoi ne pouvons-nous pas parler franchement?" (Why can't we

speak plainly?) I crossed my arms, my voice bored and borderline disrespectful. I did my best to hold the stare of the Master Jeweler, but the girl down the bar let out a squeak as the man she was with grabbed her roughly around her biceps.

I stilled.

Everything inside me quietened, heightened, and salivated.

Violence.

It always brought out the worst in me.

"Say it again. Go on. I dare you!" the man yelled in her face, shaking her. "You really want to do this? Here? Right now? When we're on holiday in fucking *Paris*?"

"I know it's not ideal, Sam, but…I've reached my limit. I just…I can't do it anymore." The girl's profile came into view as she squirmed in the guy's grip. "Just let me go, and we'll leave. We'll go somewhere quiet where we can talk and—"

"I don't want to bloody talk, Ily! That's the problem with you. That's all you want to do these days. Talk. Or take a walk. Or watch another doco on yet another stupid rock. You've turned frigid—"

"Don't you dare call me frigid. I am not—"

"Lately, you spend more time fondling your rocks than you do my cock, and frankly, I've had enough."

"Good! I've had enough too!" Her blue-black hair swung as she fought to get out of his control. "I'd much rather touch those stupid rocks than your cock any day."

"And I'd rather be with someone who has the drive to be rich and successful instead of throwing her life away wishing she was the goddamn queen so she can wear a goddamn tiara!"

"I *am* a queen, Sam. That's why I'm dumping you. You don't deserve me."

Sam let out a cruel laugh. "A queen, huh? I hate to break it to you, sweetheart, but before I came along, you were failing at all levels of life. Unwanted by the whore who birthed you, adopted by a family with more issues than most people put together, sickeningly close to your adoptive brother—which explains your lack of putting out with me: you're probably fucking him—"

She moved as fast as a viper.

Her arm was a blur as she slapped the bastard viciously hard on his pompous cheek.

The *crack* of her strike ricocheted over the heavy music, decorating his white skin with a perfect red imprint of her palm.

He froze.

She froze.

The crowd blatantly watching them gasped, and the bartender who'd given them shots rapidly poured a few more, shoving the wooden board between them as if it would stop whatever war was about to ensue.

I couldn't tear my eyes away.

I wanted to snatch the girl into my own arms and dare her to slap me the same way. I'd let her get one good hit in before I threw her on the bar, spread her legs, and feasted on the same pussy she'd denied her ex.

I'd find out for myself if she was frigid because a girl who could fight that bravely and slap that fiercely wasn't meek or weak. She was courageous—probably too much for her own good. And definitely far too much for a man like me.

Her spirit was fucking kryptonite to a man like me.

It made all the monstrous, diabolical urges inside me come dangerously alive. They snarled and howled for a single taste. For the chance to dominate—

The Master Jeweler sidestepped, blocking my view.

A low growl echoed in my chest. The urge to shove him out of the way shot down my arms before I remembered who he was and why I was here.

Family.

Future.

A cure for the sickness inside me.

Gritting my teeth, I forced a smile.

He met it with one of his own, thin and arrogant, eyes narrowed with a glint I didn't like.

"You asked why we can't speak plainly? Fine." Smiling wider, he crossed his arms and kept his voice low enough not to be overheard. "You came here seeking my approval to join my exclusive club. However, even with a personal recommendation from one of my members, you are not guaranteed access. Only proof of who you truly are will do that."

"Who I truly am?" I raised an eyebrow.

"You can't hide what you want, Henri Ward, but you also haven't given me a reason to trust you."

I stood as still and as cold as I could. "Trust isn't something you'll ever earn from me. Proof or no proof."

He chuckled. "*Bonne réponse.* (Good reply.) And you are right, of course. Trust is not something a beast can give another as the very nature of a beast is to answer to no one. Forgive me, let me word it another way." The glint in his eyes turned deadly as he swayed closer. "You want access to my Jewelry Box? Then you must convince me you are worthy."

Roland shifted beside me, throwing me a worried look. "He is worthy, Master Jeweler. I wouldn't have vouched for him if I thought—"

"Quiet, Olivan," the Jeweler snapped. "I'm only asking a trifle. After all, he wanted to speak plainly."

I crossed my arms, keeping my nervousness hidden beneath carefully controlled boredom. "Go on, then. Speak plainly. All I'm hearing is a bunch of nonsense."

The Master Jeweler laughed and slung his arm over my shoulders.

I stiffened.

My skin crawled.

But I didn't move as he whispered in my ear. "That woman. The one you can't take your eyes off. Her boyfriend just stupidly announced to anyone listening that she is far from home. She is adopted and most likely won't be missed for some time. She will be alone and in a strange city the moment that man walks away from her. She's practically penniless and will most likely be desperate to find someone to help her get home. The minute her adrenaline wears off, she'll be afraid, gullible…ripe for the taking."

He laughed blackly. "She even studies jewels as a hobby—if that's what she means by rocks. It's almost too *parfait*."

My teeth ground to dust as I fought the violent urge to shove my fist into his *parfait* nose. "*Votre point?*"

"My point, Mr Ward, is she is a jewel waiting to be mined. I want her for my collection, and you're the one who's going to get her for me."

Black, icy dread ripped through my bones. "Me?"

"*Oui*, you."

Pulling away from me, he dropped his arm, snapped his fingers at a man sulking close by in a grey suit, and clipped off a reel of French. Immediately, the unknown man passed the Master Jeweler a thick envelope.

He gave it to me as smoothly as if it were a glass of champagne.

My fingers latched around it, feeling the weight, the size, knowing instantly what it was. "Money. You're giving me money to kidnap her?"

His lips spread into a triumphant grin.

Roland laughed nervously, trying to play the same despicable game but failing.

"Oh no, *mon ami*. Nothing like that, I assure you."

The blackness pouring from the cavern within me—the abyss where I chained all manner of dastardly things—billowed darker. My cock thickened with anticipation. The ache in my blood frustrated me, irritated me, and made my rage unfurl. "What then? *Dis moi ce que tu veux?*" (What do you want from me?)

With a quirk of his eyebrow, he gave a silent command to the man in grey. The guard tipped his chin and, without any hesitation, moved to where the couple continued to argue.

He subtly broke up the watching crowd, then muttered into his wrist. The music in the club grew suspiciously louder, the lights dimmed, and darkness slithered from every corner. The garish disco balls stopped bouncing rainbows over everyone as the club sank into my personal version of hell.

The girl and her ex didn't notice, too wrapped up in their

fight.

The Master Jeweler's eyes gleamed as he looked at me. "What I want, Henri, is for you to prove you're one of us. Let go of all those restraints. Stop fighting your true nature. Step into the monster within you and embrace who you truly are." Slapping me on the back, he added, "Inside that envelope is ten thousand euros. Give it to the ex, and when he asks why, say it's payment to fuck his girlfriend."

"What?"

"He'll accept it. I guarantee it. I've been watching him while you've been watching her. He's an asshole with a poisonous ego. He wants revenge. He wants to hurt her for the embarrassment she's just caused him. Perhaps, on any other day or any other fight, he would tell you to fuck off, but not tonight. Tonight, his vanity is bruised, and he'll take the money. Not to hurt her but to prove to himself that she's nothing without him. She is *because* of him. And he's merely collecting what she owes."

"No man would willingly sell their girlfriend. Breakup or no breakup."

"He will. You have my personal guarantee."

Shit.

My pulse pounded in my veins, whooshing in my ears.

How the fuck would I survive this?

How could I control myself when this bastard was giving me the very permission I'd denied myself all my life?

Fuck, Q.

Help.

I glanced at my birdcage cufflinks, wishing they had a microphone. I wished the stranger who was my half-brother would appear and slaughter this guy now, instead of making me infiltrate a club that operated far out of the sanctity of law.

No one knew where The Jewelry Box kept their slaves.

No one ever found the men and women trafficked through it.

Once a girl or boy was targeted, they were swallowed up and never seen again.

I looked over my shoulder at the girl who'd captured my awful attention. She'd been marked. All because I'd made eye contact with her and sucked in a breath that tasted like sweetest sin.

Her life had been cut short because of *me*.

The pain she was about to endure—

I groaned.

Beneath my shame, I grew shockingly hard. Images of her submitting filled my mind while my ears throbbed with the sounds of all the screams I could wring from her.

I trembled, not because her blood would stain my hands but because I *wanted* it to.

I wanted it so fucking badly.

I was as black as this bastard beside me, and my self-control kept slipping.

Slipping…

My hands fisted around the envelope-wrapped money.

Make the choice.

Right now.

Save countless women—just like Q demanded of you—or walk away and save just one.

That one.

You don't have to do this. There isn't a gun to your head.

But at least be honest with yourself that if you refuse—the minute you say no—she's his anyway.

Breathing hard, I turned back to face the Jeweler.

Out of the two of us, I'd rather be the one to drag her into the worst nightmare of her life. With me…I would try to save her. With him…he'd make her wish for death.

He licked his lower lip, keeping a careful eye on me. "If you're worried he'll make a scene, don't be. The crowd has been dispersed. The bartender is otherwise engaged. The girl's fight has reached its end, and the boy is fuming. He knows he can't strike her. Not here at least. Yet he's plotting how to make her pay." He chuckled. "You're merely giving him revenge with a neat and tidy bow…along with a nice little payday. He'll take the money, Henri.

And when he does, you will take the girl." He pointed into the blackness. "Take her to the back of the club. There's a door. Knock four times and you'll be let inside."

Not giving me time to refuse, he stepped away. "Roland, come along. Let our new acquaintance prove he's worthy of our friendship."

Saluting me mockingly, he muttered, "Have fun, Henri. Remember. Buy the girl, bring her to me, and I promise you, your life will never be the same again."

WOULD YOU LIKE REGULAR FREE BOOKS?

Sign up to my Newsletter and receive exclusive content, deleted scenes, and freebies.

For a limited time, sign up and receive the audio book for LUNAMARE for free!

Please visit **www.pepperwinters.com** for latest updates.

Printed in Great Britain
by Amazon